The Great Mom Rescue

adapted by Natalie Shaw

based on the screenplay "Mike the Knight and the Great Rescue"

written by Rachel Dawson

Simon Spotlight

New York London Toronto Sydney New Delhi

SIMON SPOTLIGHT

An imprint of Simon & Schuster Children's Publishing Division
1230 Avenue of the Americas, New York, New York 10020
© 2014 Hit (MTK) Limited. Mike the Knight™ and logo and Be a Knight, Do It Right!™ are
trademarks of Hit (MTK) Limited. Nickelodeon and all related titles and logos are trademarks
of Viacom International Inc.

SIMON SPOTLIGHT and colophon are registered trademarks of Simon & Schuster, Inc.
For information about special discounts for bulk purchases, please contact Simon & Schuster
Special Sales at 1-866-506-1949 or business@simonandschuster.com.
Manufactured in The United States 0214 LAK
First Edition 10 9 8 7 6 5 4 3 2 1
ISBN 978-1-4424-9605-7
ISBN 978-1-4424-9606-4 (eBook)

Mike has two dragons.
They like to have fun.
The big one is chasing
the little one!
Now Mike has to save
Squirt from Sparkie's flame,
to show he's the best
at this rescue game!

Mike and his dragon friends were playing in the castle yard.
They were pretending that Sparkie had captured Squirt, and
that Mike was a brave knight coming to the rescue.

"Stand back, fierce dragon!" Mike yelled at Sparkie. Then,
pretending a soup ladle was a sword, he poked Sparkie in the
stomach.

"Roar!" yelled Sparkie. "You got me! I surrender!"

"I wonder what it's like to be a real rescuer?" Mike said.
"I'm Mike the Knight, and my mission is to *really* rescue someone!"

Mike put on his armor and drew his sword. But instead of a sword, there was a carrot!

"How can I use a carrot to rescue someone?" Mike wondered.

"If anyone can find a way, Mike, you can!" said Squirt.

They all raced to the village to find someone to rescue.

No one needed help, so Mike grabbed his *Big Book for Little Knights in Training* and read the page about rescuing.

"It says to remember these steps: Listen, look, ask . . . then rescue!" said Mike. "And it shows a knight rescuing a princess!"

While they were waiting for a real rescue, Sparkie and Squirt dressed up like princesses and pretended that Mike's horse, Galahad, was a bad guy.

"Help! Help! Save me from this scary beast!" yelled Sparkie.

They climbed into a cart, pretending it was the tower they had seen in Mike's book.

"Fear not, Lady Sparkie and Lady Squirt!" Mike yelled. "I'll save you!"

Then Mike thought he heard a woman scream. It sounded like someone *really* needed rescuing!

Mike ran to help, dashing through the clotheslines, and sending bedsheets and bloomers flying. But the woman didn't need to be rescued after all.

"I wasn't screaming," she explained. "I was singing!"

Then Mike heard Mrs. Piecrust yelling and saw smoke
coming from the bakery, followed by crashes and bangs!
"Mrs. Piecrust must need to be rescued!" he said.
He ran into the bakery to help.

"Watch out for my pies!" Mrs. Piecrust hollered as Mike ran in and knocked them over, sending them rolling out the door.

"But I heard you yelling and saw smoke. I thought you needed to be rescued," Mike explained.

"Rescued? I burnt a pie, that's all," said Mrs. Piecrust.

Just then, Queen Martha and her dogs, Yip and Yap,
entered the square. The dogs started to yip and yap at a pie
that rolled under the cart.

"Yip! Yap! Leave that pie alone," shouted the queen. But the
dogs pulled on their leashes, dragging the queen onto the back
of the cart alongside Sparkie and Squirt.

The dogs' yapping spooked the cart horse! It reared on its hind legs and bolted . . .

. . . pulling the cart behind it, and taking the queen, Sparkie, and Squirt along for the ride.

"Ahhh!" yelled Queen Martha.

"Whoa!" yelled Sparkie.

"Help!" yelled Squirt. But the cart horse wouldn't stop.

"Uh-oh!" Mike said. "It *looks* like they need rescuing. It *sounds* like they need rescuing. But this time, I'll *ask* them, too. It's time to be a knight, and do it right!"

Mike yelled after the cart. "Mom! Sparkie! Squirt! Do you need to be rescued?"

"Yes!" they all yelled as the cart horse took them farther and farther away.

"Mike the Knight to the rescue!" Mike yelled.
He leaped onto Galahad, and they galloped toward the cart until they caught up. Then Mike hopped from Galahad onto the cart horse's back.

"Whoa, boy! Slow down!" Mike said to the cart horse, but the cart horse wouldn't stop. It was headed straight for the castle moat! And the drawbridge was up! Mike was running out of time. Then he had an idea.

"Look, horsey!" Mike said, dangling the carrot in front of the cart horse's nose.

As Mike raised the carrot, the cart horse lifted its head, and when Mike moved the carrot to the left, the cart horse moved to the left too, away from the moat. It worked!

Finally, Mike yanked the carrot up and the cart horse
slowed down and stopped! Mike hopped off of the cart horse
and gave him the carrot to eat while the queen, Sparkie, and
Squirt climbed out of the cart.

"Huzzah!" they all yelled.
"You rescued us, Mike!
I'm so proud of you!" Queen
Martha said.

"Thanks, Mom. It's because I
remembered to look, listen, ask,
then rescue, like a real knight!"

Now that the real rescue was over, they headed back to the village. Sparkie went to the bakery to help Mrs. Piecrust bake more pies . . .

. . . and Mike and Squirt helped with the laundry. After all, it was the knightly thing to do!